Library of Congress catalog card number: 81-67667
ISBN 0-689-50230-3
Copyright © 1981 by Iris Schweitzer
All rights reserved
Printed in Great Britain
First American Edition

HILDA'S RESTFUL CHAIR

Iris Schweitzer

A Margaret K. McElderry Book
Atheneum   1982   New York

It was a hot morning.
Hilda finished watering the
vegetable garden.
She turned the water off and rolled
up the hose.
"I'm exhausted," she said.

"Me too," said Osbert, the wombat. Lying in the shade, he sighed; he had been snoozing, but water had splashed on his eyelids and woken him up.

"It's a hard life," he said to himself.

Hilda patted her hot cheeks with her wet hands.

"And now for a little cool and quiet in my restful chair," she said, walking over to the shed where she kept her old armchair.

Osbert yawned and stretched.
Then he got up, and with his eyes
still half-closed, he followed Hilda.
But when Hilda got to the restful
chair, she found Cadbury the cat in
it, sprawled across the entire seat.

"Excuse me," said Hilda, pushing Cadbury to one side.

"There," she said, and getting into the chair, she made herself comfortable.

"What about me?" asked Osbert.

"Oh, come on then," said Hilda, and lifted him into the chair.

The chair creaked.

"Peace at last," thought Hilda.
But just then Cream and Smiles,
the two bunnies, came in. They
were always together.
"We are so exhausted," they said
politely. "May we rest a little in
your restful chair?"
"Oh, all right," said Hilda.
And she picked them up and made
room for them.

The chair creaked some more.

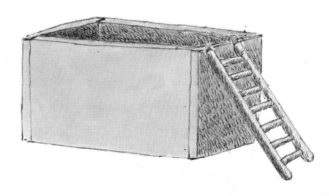

Hilda had hardly settled down,
when Chester the badger arrived.
He lived in the woods nearby, and
liked to visit.
"I'm so tired," he said. "Would you
mind?"
"Not *another* one!" sighed Hilda.
Chester, however, without waiting
for an answer, climbed up and
squeezed himself into the crowded
chair.
"Welcome," said Hilda, half-
heartedly.

The chair creaked
and groaned.

Two minutes later, Ivan the duck turned up. Without so much as an "excuse me" or a "may I", he hopped up and perched on the arm of the chair. The bunnies moved closer together. Osbert grunted but did not open his eyes. The badger didn't budge.

"Glad you could make it," muttered Hilda. "All I need now is a few chickens and a sheep."

The chair creaked and groaned even more.

And as if all that wasn't enough, Lightfoot the field mouse decided to join the party. She streaked up the chair and stopped at the top. First she gave her whiskers a bit of a clean. Then she curled up and started dreaming.

THE WAS THE LAST STRAW FOR THE CHAIR!

It overturned, and everybody
tumbled out!
They fell over each other, and
bumped into each other, and their
heads and feet got all mixed up.

But as soon as they felt that nothing hurt, they broke out into a great cackle.

"Ooh-ooh-ooh, eeh-eeh-eeh! That was a good rest we had!" they shouted. "It's time we went home now."

And off they went.

"There, Old Restful," said Hilda, as she stood the chair back up. "Everybody's gone."

"Not quite everybody," said Osbert. "Oh good," said Hilda. Because it was nice to have one friend stay. "And as we didn't get much cool and quiet," she continued, "how about some cool sweet watermelon instead?" Osbert thought that a very good idea. So they walked back to the house and into the kitchen, where, by some magic, they found two slices of watermelon all ready for them.

1